# Usborne
# 1001
# Fairy
# things to spot
# Sticker Book

D0762725

Gillian Doherty
Illustrated by Teri Gower

Designed by Teri Gower and Doriana Berkovic
Cover design by Nelupa Hussain
Edited by Anna Milbourne

# Contents

# Things to spot

Fairyland is a magical place where just about anything can happen, and often does. Each scene in this book has all kinds of wonderful and surprising things for you to find and count. There are 1001 things to spot altogether.

Moon dance

10 white rabbits

6 pixies on toadstools

1 full moon

9 fairies with sparkly wings

7 shooting stars

10 fairy lanterns

2 snowy owls

8 glow-worms

1 unicorn

2 golden slippers

Each little faded picture shows you what to look for in the big picture.

The number by each faded picture shows how many of that thing you need to find.

When you've found all of each thing, put a matching sticker on top of the faded picture. You'll find the stickers in the middle of the book.

Dizzy Rainbow is new in fairyland and is busy discovering its secrets. Can you find her in every scene?

# Fairy feast

**10** leaf trays

**9** bowls of marshmallows

**10** sugar mice

**9** blackberry tarts

**8** yellow bows

**7** paper garlands

**10** strawberry drinks

**9** fairy cakes

**1** greedy goblin

**8** plates of star cookies

# Enchanted waterfall

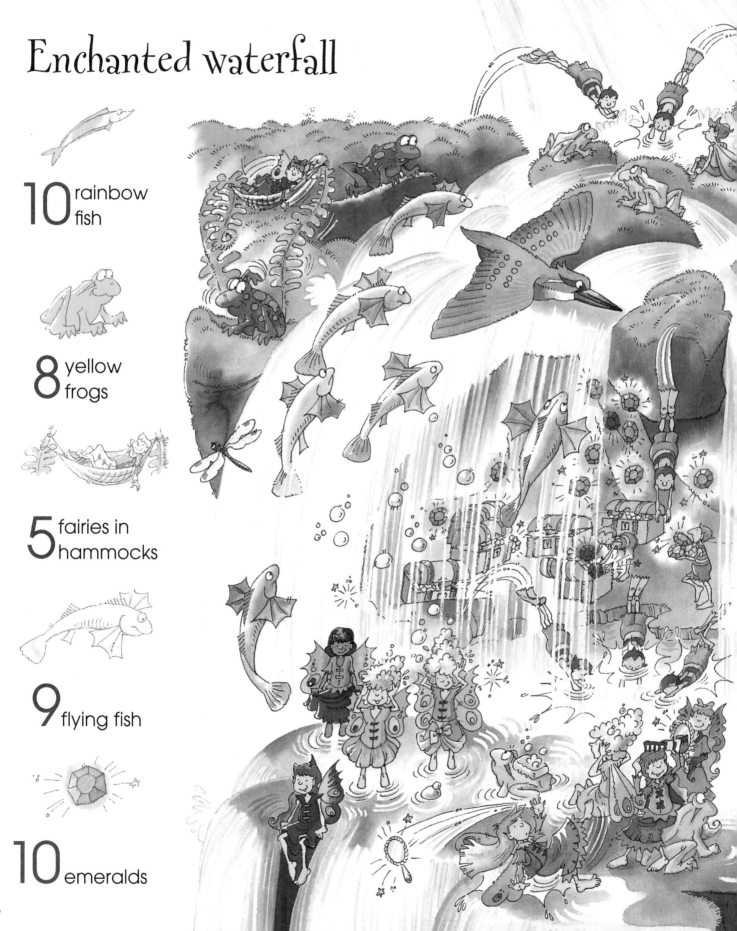

10 rainbow fish

8 yellow frogs

5 fairies in hammocks

9 flying fish

10 emeralds

**2** kingfishers

**3** fairies washing their hair

**5** mirrors

**7** treasure chests

**6** elves diving for jewels

7

# Moon dance

**7** shooting stars

**10** white rabbits

**6** pixes on toadstools

**1** full moon

**9** fairies with sparkly wings

**10** fairy lanterns    **2** snowy owls    **8** glow-worms    **1** unicorn    **2** golden slippers

# Fairy school

7 fairies having flying lessons

6 writing quills

10 purple beetles

3 pumpkin coaches

8 spell books

**10** magic wands

**9** white mice

**5** frog princes

**1** baby dragon

**8** pink snails

11

# Magic market

 **10** jars of fairy kisses

 **9** candy canes

 **7** petal parasols

 **7** rainbow cauldrons

 **9** wizard hats

8 spell scrolls

4 flying carpets

10 book worms

8 magic lamps

10 boxes of wishes

# Secret garden

**10** dandelion clocks

**4** fairies splashing

**9** dragonflies

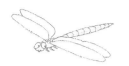
**5** daisy chains

**9** yellow butterflies

**8** striped caterpillars

**10** bluebells

**7** yellow flower fairies

**8** elves riding snails

15

# Fairy palace

**10** striped fish

**7** spotted turtles

**10** pink flags

**8** mermaids

**7** boats with leaf sails

Use these stickers on pages 4-5.

Use these stickers on pages 6-7.

Use these stickers on pages 8-9.

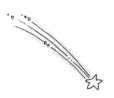    

Use these stickers on pages 10-11.

Use these stickers on pages 12-13.

Use these stickers on pages 14-15.

Use these stickers on pages 16-17.

Use these stickers on pages 18-19.

Use these stickers on pages 20-21.

Use these stickers on pages 22-23.

Use these stickers on pages 24-25.

Use these stickers on pages 26-27.

Use these stickers on pages 28-29.

Use these stickers on pages 30-31.

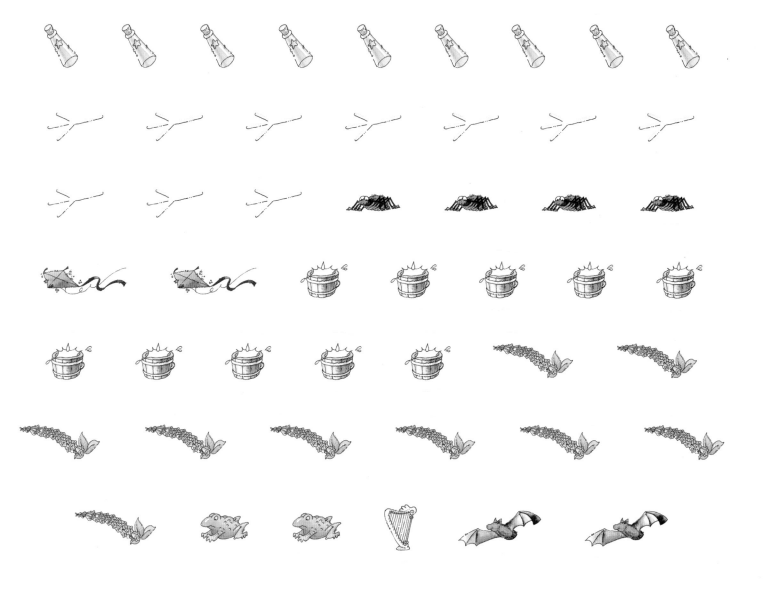

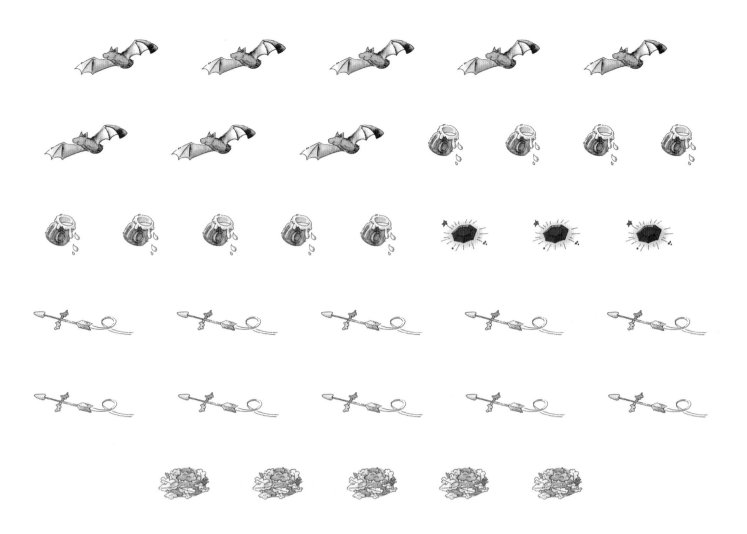

You could reward yourself by sticking one of these stickers on every page when you've found all the things around the edges.

**8** nutshell boats

**10** fairy horses

**9** elf archers

**6** pearls

**8** goblin guards

# House fairies

**8** striped socks

**6** spotted socks

**10** pink buttons

**1** sleepy cat

**10** spools of thread

 **9** blue pins

 **7** fairies sewing

 **9** star buttons

 **5** fairies bouncing

**7** cobweb dresses

# Rainbow fairies

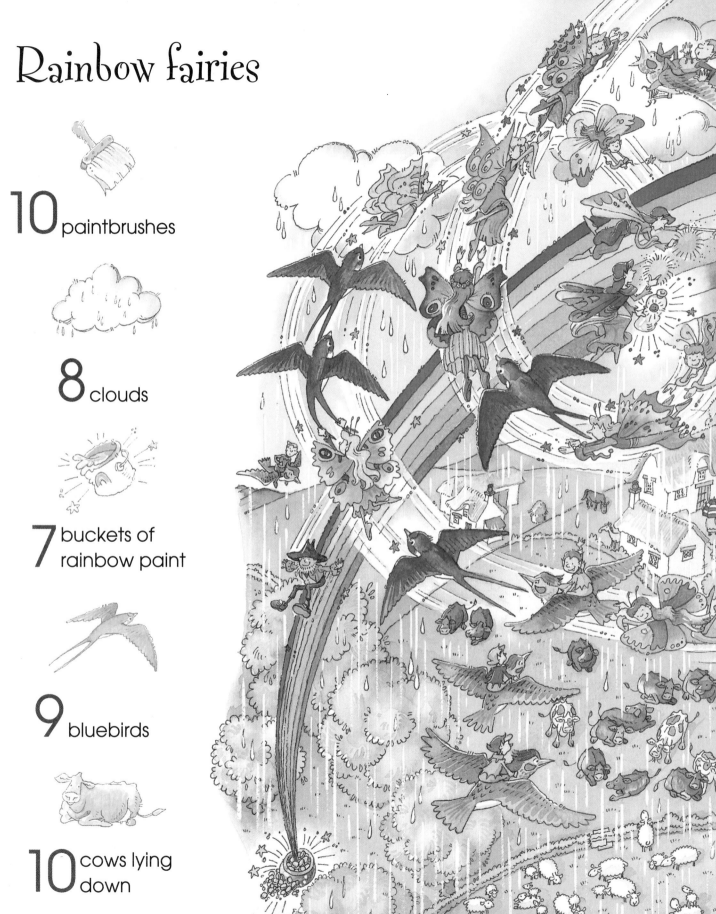

**10** paintbrushes

**8** clouds

**7** buckets of
rainbow paint

**9** bluebirds

**10** cows lying
down

1 leprechaun

8 striped umbrellas

9 pixies riding on skylarks

1 pot of gold

10 chimney pots

# Treetop fairies

**2** red squirrels

**5** pixies climbing ladders

**9** moths

**10** round windows

**3** dormice sleeping

22

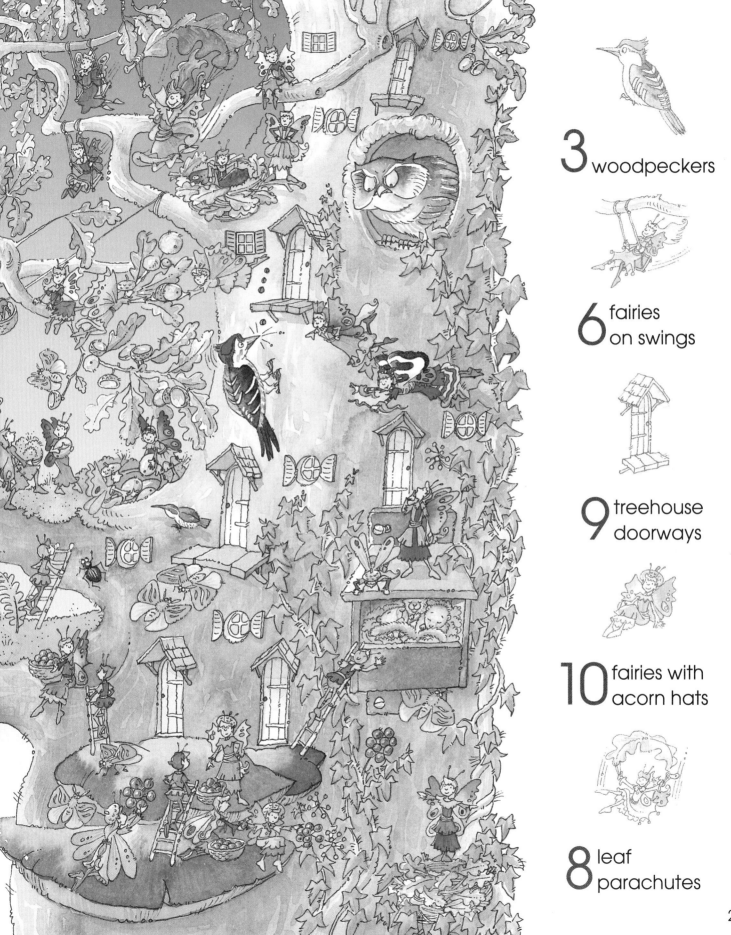

3 woodpeckers

6 fairies on swings

9 treehouse doorways

10 fairies with acorn hats

8 leaf parachutes

23

# Fairy treehouse

9 candles

7 marbles

3 fairy newspapers

9 building blocks

8 feather dusters

24

 **6** baby fairies

 **4** self-flipping pancakes

 **1** pink rabbit

 **10** flyaway letters

 **2** snow fairies

# Fairyland workshop

**4** elves with red boxes

**6** blue balloons

**10** spotted bow ties

**7** toy trains

**9** fairy hammers

**10** striped balls

**1** jack-in-a-box

**3** fairies pulling levers

**7** pouches of fairy dust

**8** teddy bears

# The Snow Queen's ball

**7** fairies with fluffy hats

**3** ice thrones

**9** goblets of fairy punch

**10** snowballs

**3** golden crowns

2 golden bowls

8 red mittens

10 fairies ice-skating

1 crystal chandelier

7 snow hares

# Dizzy Rainbow's magic spells

Dizzy Rainbow is at fairy school, and she needs all kinds of strange things for her magic class. Look back through the book to help her find them all, and add a sticker here for each thing that you find.

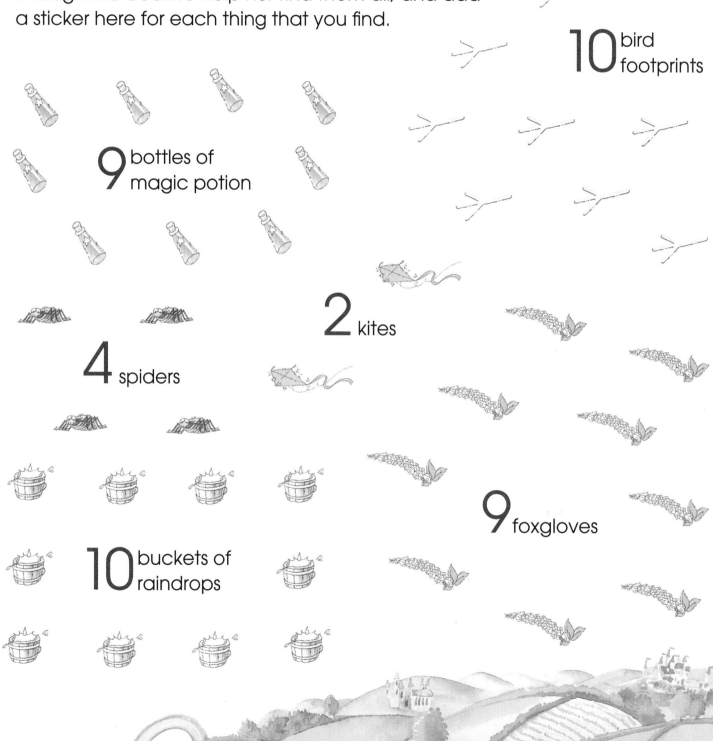

**10** bird footprints

**9** bottles of magic potion

**2** kites

**4** spiders

**9** foxgloves

**10** buckets of raindrops

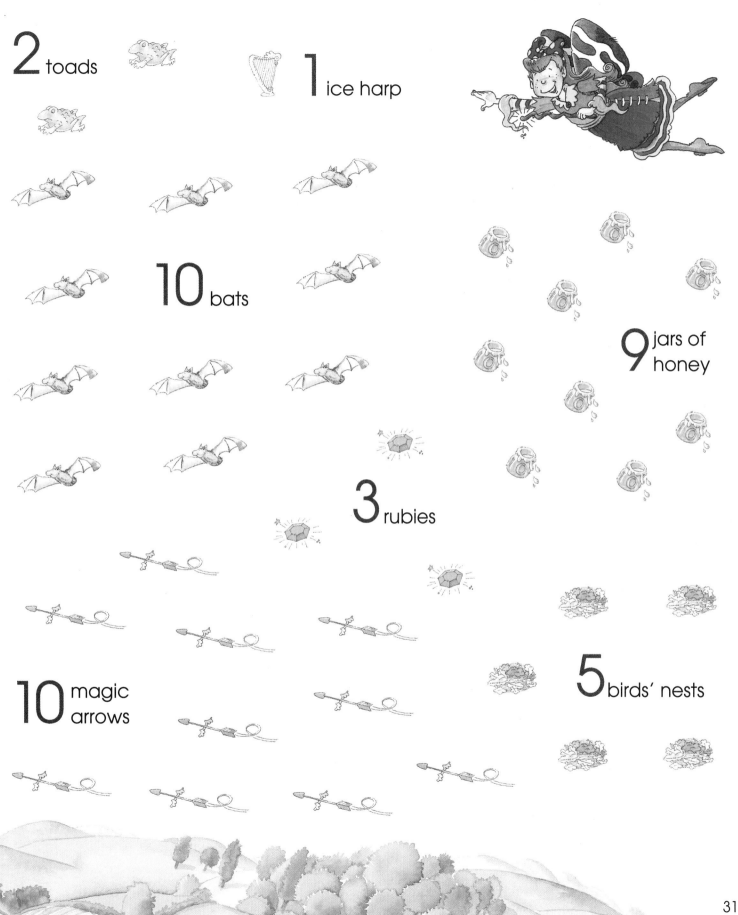

2 toads

1 ice harp

10 bats

9 jars of honey

3 rubies

5 birds' nests

10 magic arrows

# Answers

Did you find all the things Dizzy Rainbow needs
for her magic class? Here's where they are:

9 bottles of magic potion
Magic market
(pages 12-13)

9 jars of honey
Fairy feast
(pages 4-5)

10 buckets of raindrops
Rainbow fairies
(pages 20-21)

5 birds' nests
Treetop fairies
(pages 22-23)

10 bird footprints
Fairy treehouse
(pages 24-25)

10 bats
Moon dance
(pages 8-9)

4 spiders
House fairies
(pages 18-19)

10 magic arrows
Fairy palace
(pages 16-17)

3 rubies
Enchanted waterfall
(pages 6-7)

9 foxgloves
Secret garden
(pages 14-15)

2 kites
Fairyland workshop
(pages 26-27)

2 toads
Fairy school
(pages 10-11)

1 ice harp
The Snow Queen's ball
(pages 28-29)

First published in 2014 by Usborne Publishing Ltd.,
Usborne House, 83-85 Saffron Hill, London EC1N 8RT, England. www.usborne.com